CAN YOU SEE ME?

CAN YOU SEE ME?

Mikhala Lantz-Simmons
Mohammad Rasoulipour

Andrews McMeel
PUBLISHING®

My large antlers can be a bother
as I make my way
from the woods to the water.

Can you see me?

We baaah and bleat
when it's time to eat.

But can you see us?

Through the bush I sneak.
My bushy tail follows my leap.

Can you see me?

I chew on bamboo.
There's nothing else to do.

Can you see me?

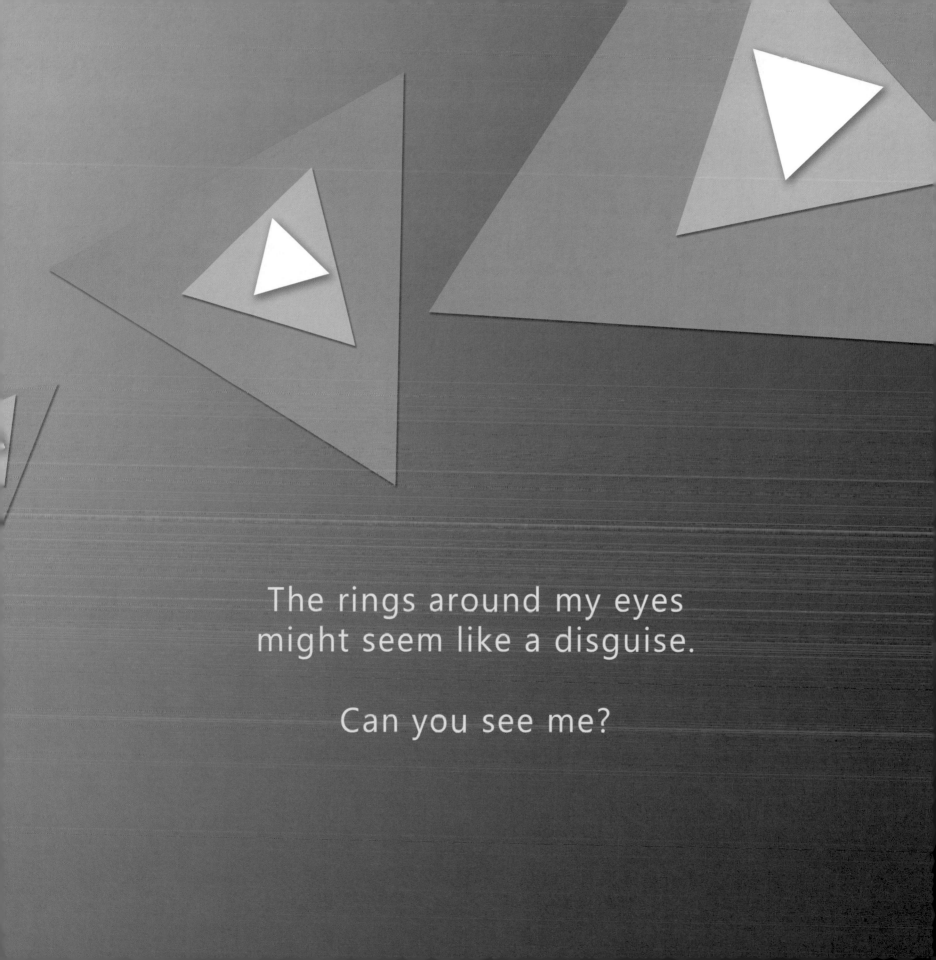

The rings around my eyes
might seem like a disguise.

Can you see me?

I spray my smelly scent
as a sign of discontent.

Can you see me?

I use sound to navigate around.

Can you see me?

My bright eyes blink
as the sun starts to sink.

Can you see me?

I surf through the water.
Once on land,
my flippers make me totter.

Can you see me?

My tusks are nice
for poking holes up through the ice.

But can you see me?

I have lines of sharp, shiny teeth,
up top, in back,
and underneath.

Can you see me?

I slide through the swamp,
ready to chomp.

Can you see me?

I eat from the tops of trees
and do as I please.

Can you see me?

The savanna is my home,
where I royally roam.

Can you see me?

I have two horns on my face,
such an obvious place.

Can you see me?

I curl up in your lap,
ready for a nap.

Can you see me?

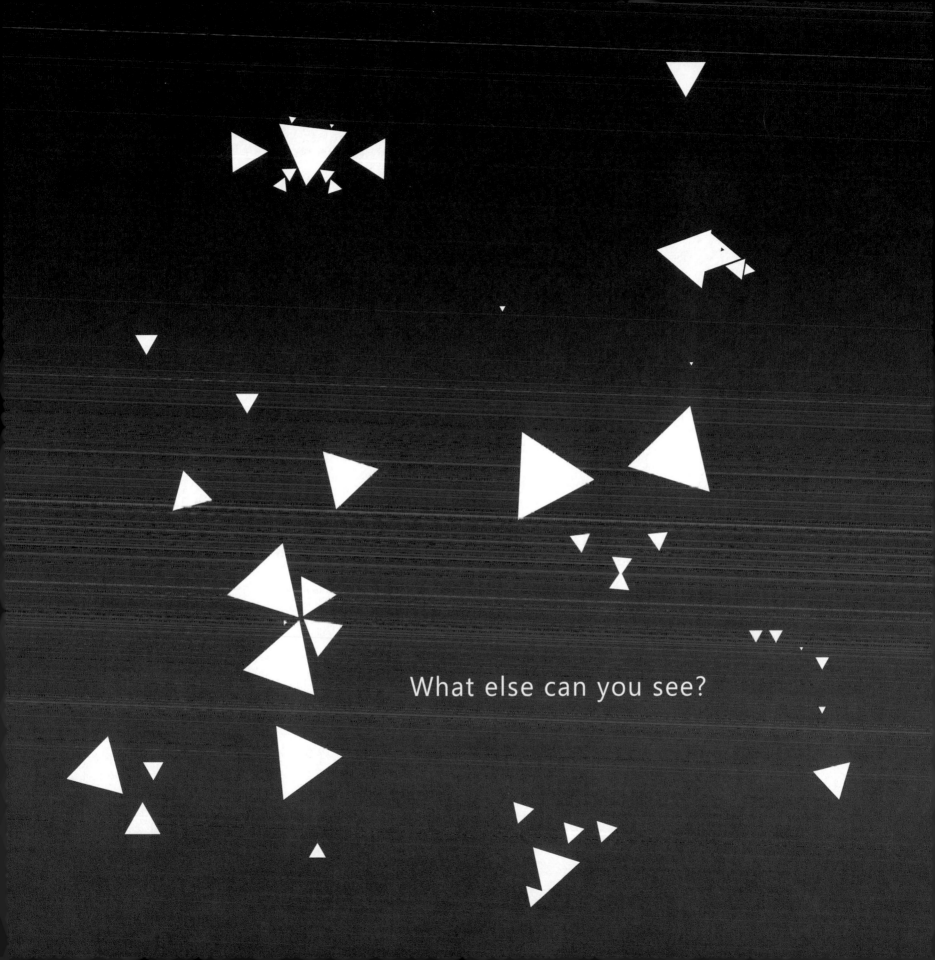

What else can you see?

ABOUT THE AUTHORS

Mikhala Lantz-Simmons and Mohammad Rasoulipour
are a married couple who met while studying
peacebuilding in the Shenandoah Valley. At home,
they like to speak their made-up language
and do art projects together.

Thanks to the curious kids who
helped make this into a book:
Parsa, Sydney, Ragad,
Ghaida, and Wynne.

CAN YOU SEE ME?

Andrews McMeel Publishing
a division of Andrews McMeel Universal
1130 Walnut Street, Kansas City, Missouri 64106

www.andrewsmcmeel.com

19 20 21 22 23 TEN 10 9 8 7 6 5 4 3 2 1

ISBN: 978-1-5248-5372-3

Made by:
1010 Printing International, Ltd.
Address and place of production:
1010 Avenue, Xia Nan Industrial District,
Yuan Zhou Town, Bo Luo County
Guangdong Province, China 516123
1st printing – 7/15/19

Editor: Melissa Rhodes Zahorsky
Art Director/Designer: Julie Barnes
Production Editor: Margaret Daniels
Production Manager: Tamara Haus